Written by Susan Nicholson
Illustrated by Kirsten Richards

This edition published by Parragon in 2009

Parragon
Queen Street House
4 Queen Street
Bath BA1 1HE, UK

ISBN 978-1-4075-5098-5

Printed in China

I Love My Kitten!

Bath · New York · Singapore · Hong Kong · Cologne · Delhi · Melbourne

Emily went to visit her grandma every weekend. Grandma's house was very pretty, with roses growing around the front door and a big yard at the back.

It was also full of cats—lots of cats...

There were three fluffy cats with long, silky fur:

Kitty...   Empress Amelia...   and Lady Sue.

There were twin cats called Kiki and Coco.
They had bright blue eyes and short, sleek coats.

There was Duchess, a bluish-gray cat with large pointed ears and tiny oval paws.

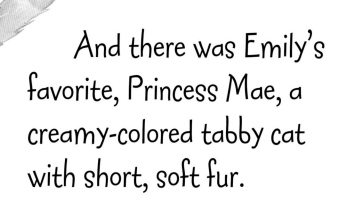

And there was Emily's favorite, Princess Mae, a creamy-colored tabby cat with short, soft fur.

Emily loved to help Grandma look after the cats. First, her grandma would give the cats their food. Each cat had its own special bowl.

Then Emily helped Grandma to groom them. The fluffy cats needed their long hair brushing at least once every day.

Princess Mae could lick her own fur clean because it was much shorter. But she still loved to sit on Emily's knee, purring softly, while Emily combed her creamy coat.

Sometimes, Grandma entered her cats in special cat shows. They had won lots of prizes.

Emily loved to look at all the photographs and trophies.

"Princess Mae won a trophy when she was just eight months old," explained Grandma.

The following weekend, Grandma had some exciting news. Princess Mae was going to have kittens!

"Would you like to choose one of Princess Mae's kittens for your very own?"

"Oh, yes, please," gasped Emily, with shining eyes.

"You'll have to be patient. The kittens won't be here for another month or so, and then they'll have to stay with their mom until they are around ten weeks old."

Emily's face fell. "Do I really have to wait that long?" she asked.

"I know that seems like a long time, but it will fly by," said Grandma. Emily nodded glumly.

One day, Emily went round to help her grandma prepare for the new arrivals. They had bought a basket and covered it with an old blanket.

"Princess Mae can have her kittens in here," explained Grandma. "It's warm and dry, and she'll feel safe."

Princess Mae seemed to know at once that the basket was for her.

"Oh, and I've got something for you, Emily," said Grandma, and she handed Emily a little box. Inside was a pretty silver necklace with a tiny kitten charm.

"Oh thank you, Grandma. It's lovely!" cried Emily giving Grandma a hug.

"You can wear it to remind you of the kitten you'll soon have to cherish," smiled Grandma.

The next time Emily went to visit, Grandma was
waiting at the door.

"Princess Mae's
kittens have arrived!"

Emily and Grandma crept quietly
into the kitchen. There, curled up beside
Princess Mae, were five tiny, furry kittens.
"They're beautiful!" said Emily softly.

"When can I pick one?" whispered Emily.

"Whenever you like," replied Grandma, "but it's best to wait until they are older, then you'll know for sure which one you want."

At first, the kittens spent most of their time curled up next to Princess Mae, drinking her milk or sleeping.

Then, after a week or so, they began to crawl.

One stripy little kitten
crawled right across the floor
to sniff Emily's hand.

After two weeks, the kittens began to explore.

Emily was at her grandma's baking some cakes when the same stripy little kitten came over and tried to join in.

When they were four
weeks old, the kittens began
to grow teeth.

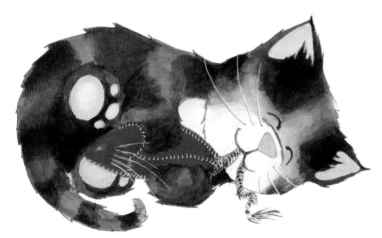

The stripy little kitten
especially loved playing with
the red chewing toy that Emily
had bought.

By the time the kittens were six weeks old, they were racing around and playing with each other.

Princess Mae was kept very busy looking after them. Luckily, the other cats helped, too.

"I think you've chosen your favorite," smiled Grandma one day as she watched the stripy little kitten playing with Emily's charm necklace.

"I think she's chosen me," laughed Emily. "I'm going to call her Tiger Mae—after Princess Mae and because of her striped fur!"

"And she seems to like my necklace. Every time I wear it, it reminds me that she was worth waiting for."

A few weeks later, the kittens were old enough to leave their mother. Emily brought a cat basket to Grandma's so she could carry Tiger Mae home.

The other kittens were going to live with some of Grandma's friends. "That way, we'll be able to visit them," explained Grandma, tickling Princess Mae's ears.

"Yes, and I'll bring Tiger Mae to visit, too," said Emily.

"Grandma, do you think I could enter Tiger Mae in cat shows when she's older?" asked Emily.

"Yes," replied Grandma, smiling. "You've learned a lot about looking after cats. I think that would be a very good idea!"

"Do you hear that, Tiger Mae?" whispered Emily. "Maybe one day we'll win a big gold cup, just like Princess Mae."

And a little while later…they did!